ANGEL AND THE NEVILLE NEXT DOOR

NEXT DOOR

FRIENDSHIP, LOVE AND SECOND CHANCES

JEANINE LAUREN

Littleford House Books

ISBN 978-1-9990707-8-6

CHAPTER 1

Helen Baker peeked out from behind her heavy living-room drapes to the darkened street, surveying the space between the streetlights. She hadn't seen any ghosts or witches or Star Wars characters in at least thirty minutes. The mantel clock—a wedding present for her and Sam thirty years earlier—struck eight, and she let the drapes drop back into place.

Halloween was over, and so was the most hellish year of her life.

She shut off the front porch light and carried the bowl with the remaining miniature chocolate bars to the kitchen. There were enough of these sweet morsels to give her a sugar high. She should put them away, but she had earned the right to celebrate first.

A bottle of her favorite Merlot, which she had found the last time she went wine tasting in the Okanagan, waited patiently on the kitchen table along with a large goblet, her day planner, a red marker, and the sealed manila envelope she had received earlier that day. She peeled the wrapping off a chocolate, popped it into her mouth, and poured the wine. She sat down at the table and, ignoring the envelope, opened the book.

Taking up a red pen, she marked off the day with an X. Then she lifted the glass and toasted herself.

"Well, Helen, congratulations. You

did it." She had kept her promise to her mother and her therapist and had managed to get through the gauntlet of firsts: first Christmas, first birthday, first Valentine's Day, first wedding anniversary, first major family occasion—in this case, their daughter's wedding—and now her first Halloween without her husband by her side. Promise kept, she could move on to her new life, alone, on her own terms.

The crackle and pop of fireworks made her jump, and then her blood pressure rose. They weren't holding a Halloween party. Not after last year's shenanigans, surely?

She looked out the window and her eyes confirmed what her ears were hearing. There was Jillian, her former best friend, all bright-eyed smiles, showing off her new haircut and slimmer figure and entertaining all their neighbors without her. Seriously? Did she feel no remorse at all?

Helen tromped to the front door, pulled on her coat and shoes, crammed a toque on her head, and grabbed her gloves. She would go over there and give Jill a piece of her mind. How dare she hold the party they had always held together? How dare she entertain the neighbors without her? She would go over there, and...

And then what?

Repeat last year's disgrace?

Tears pricked at her eyes, and she stopped with her hand on the doorknob. She had celebrated too soon this evening. She had one more first to get through before she could really move on. She walked to the kitchen window and watched the bright yellow, red, and green fireworks sail upward, pause, burst into hundreds of bits of light, and then fall back to earth. This was the first time in twenty-three years she wasn't part of this neighborhood tradition.

It had started when Kim and Brandon —her daughter and Jillian's son—were five. Helen and Jillian, who lived next door to each other, took turns holding the backyard Halloween fireworks party. Even after Kim had grown and moved away from Vancouver Island to attend school in Toronto, Helen and Jillian continued to hold the party. To offer this fun for other children helped ease the emptiness that came from their children moving on. Even after Jill's husband died two years earlier, they continued to hold it. Just the same as always... until last year.

Last year, another neighbor, Khalid, had insisted on putting on the fireworks. He had an extra-special display, he'd said, and had gotten the fireworks on sale.

Helen and her husband, Sam, had been happy to pass the torch.

The finale had been spectacular, lighting up the sky much brighter than in previous years. It also exposed the shadows—including the one Jillian and Sam were canoodling in, unaware they had been caught. Helen tromped over to the back of the shed, where they were nearly fornicating in public, and screamed at them. Thankfully, the shadows had returned by then, and the noise from the crowd was enough to drown out most of her anguish. Anyone who saw them worked hard to pretend they hadn't, and most guests made their excuses to leave, slinking into the night quickly.

"It meant nothing," Sam insisted later.

"It just happened," said Jill.

But things like that don't just happen, and once the fireworks had exposed their affair, she saw the other things that had been hiding in dark places: the mutual friends who couldn't look her in the eye, the money disappearing from their joint account, the fact that Jill would coincidentally visit her mother every time Sam had to go out of town for a meeting. They were the indisputable signs of a decaying marriage and, worse, a decaying friendship.

She couldn't and wouldn't replay that scene today. She stripped off her coat and boots and traipsed back to the kitchen. She topped off her wineglass and took that and her planner into the dining room, as far away from the fireworks and joyful noise as she could get. She was truly alone now.

In the past year, she had seen the friends drift away. They offered excuses for not seeing her, as though she had leprosy and not a case of singleness. To be single in a world of couples was to be a thorn amongst roses. Dangerous. Suspect. Alone.

Despite her loneliness, she had done well managing the year of firsts. She rarely cried and just kept going: teaching, planning Kim's wedding, facing each morning with courage, and ending each day tired but with a sense of accomplishment. Why, after getting through all those tough days in one piece, was she now standing in her dining room, sobbing?

She glanced at the unopened envelope again: the divorce papers her lawyer had sent over by courier. All she had to do was sign them.

The phone rang, then, and she stood up, swiping at the tears with her sleeve as she walked back to the kitchen to retrieve her cell phone.

"Hello?"

"Hello, Helen. It's Sylvia. I wanted to

call and see how you were doing. I remember..." She paused a moment. "Well, it's been a year, and I just wanted to see how you're getting on."

"Oh, Sylvia, thank you for calling." Helen leaned over to grab a tissue from a nearby box and mop up her tears. "It is so good to hear from you."

"I also wanted to invite you to visit on the next long weekend in November. I know you wanted a reason to get back here one day."

Sylvia was right. Helen had been meaning to spend some time in Sunshine Bay. It had been a vacation spot for her family when she was a child. Later, she and Kim had spent summer vacations at a cabin on the beach there. Sam hadn't ever been able to join them, preferring vacations that involved flying. It made Sunshine Bay a place for just the two of them, and right now she wanted to visit somewhere that wasn't soaked in memories of Sam.

"That would be nice. I would give me a reason to get away."

"That's great," said Sylvia. "And if you like it here, well..."

"Is there something else?"

"Actually," Sylvia said, "there *is* something else. I know Kim is staying in Ontario for the holidays this year, and you said you didn't have any firm plans..."

No, Helen didn't want to spend Christmas with Sylvia and Jack. It would just remind her she was a third wheel.

"Oh, Sylvia, that's sweet. But I was planning to go somewhere like Tofino and spend some time watching storms or something. You know. Alone and doing something that doesn't involve Christmas in Duncan."

"What? No. I think you

misunderstand me. And I feel strange for asking, but..."

"But what? Do you need something?"

"Well... I know this is a lot to ask—"

"More so than when I asked you to help with Kim's wedding? I'll do anything I can to help. What do you need?" Sylvia had stood by her, a rock in the stream of emotions leading up to Kim's big day. If there was any way she could help, she would. Sylvia had been someone she could count on when those she had counted on before had floated out of reach.

"I hoped that you would consider spending your time in Sunshine Bay, house-sitting for Jack and me. Well, cat-sitting. We plan to visit Jack's daughter Cassie in Kelowna. Angel would need to stay here, and it'll be the first time I've left her since she began to trust us."

"Hence the visit next weekend?"

"You caught me. I thought it would solve two problems at once: it would give you a place to go, and it would also help me. You're good with animals, and I know what it's like to spend Christmas alone. After my first husband died, I didn't want to see anyone."

"Yes. And I would love to watch over Angel for Christmas. It will give me time to figure out what to do next." She couldn't stay here, and Sunshine Bay had always intrigued her. It was larger than Duncan but still had that small-town feeling. And it was far away from neighbors and friends who no longer saw her as part of their life. Maybe Sunshine Bay could be more than a place to spend Christmas. Maybe it could be a place where she could create a new life. Where she could finally belong.

"Wonderful," said Sylvia. "When

does school end this semester? I'm afraid I am out of the loop these days."

"For me, it's over two weeks before Christmas. I've been filling in for a teacher who had surgery. She will return to the classroom part-time within the next three weeks and then full-time in mid-December."

"Well, when you get here this weekend, we can talk about a good day for you to come back."

"That sounds grand. I'll see you in two weeks. I'll head up directly after school, so I should be there just in time for dinner."

It was too bad Sylvia had a cat and not a dog, Helen thought, but she supposed it was better than nothing. Maybe she could coax this cat to spend some time with her. Sam's cat now lived next door. She never did get along with that animal, and now she knew why the cat had always welcomed Jillian whenever she came to visit.

Even her cat had been a traitor, but she couldn't blame Angel for that. Besides, this cat-sitting adventure would only be for two weeks.

CHAPTER 2

oe Brooks stood on the curb with his daughter-in-law, Nicole. They were in front of his house in Sunshine Bay, watching his son Zachary lift a suitcase into the back of the taxi. It was really true. The pair was off to Nicaragua for at least three months.

"Goodbye," Nicole said in a voice higher than normal. She was crouched at Joe's knee, talking to Neville, her West Highland white terrier. "I'm going to miss you, baby."

Joe turned his attention toward Zac, who stepped up beside him on the curb.

"Bye, Dad," Zac said, leaning forward to hug Joe. "I'll miss you."

"Good luck with your project. I'm sure it will be a grand adventure."

"Yeah, we're looking forward to it." Zac stepped back. "Nic, it's time to go."

Nicole gave Neville a last pat on the head. "You be a good boy for Joe." Then she turned and hugged Joe. "We'll miss you."

"You have a good time down there. It's a terrific opportunity."

Zac gave him another hug. "Thanks for taking care of Neville. Nic was more worried about him than about the trip."

"Not a problem," Joe said, swallowing down a lump in his throat. He hadn't expected to feel emotional over this. The two had been living in Vancouver for several years now, and Joe rarely saw his son unless he took the time to go to the mainland himself. But it felt different knowing they would be thousands of miles away working on an environmental project. It was a heck of a lot farther than a ferry ride.

He watched the cab until it rounded the corner, then stared at the end of the street for a few moments longer. He would miss Zac, especially next month. It would be the first time since Zac was born twenty-seven years before that they would not be spending Christmas together.

A small yap from below turned his attention downward. *Neville.* This was the other reason he was going to miss his son. Neville was a cute little thing, and the subject of much oohing and ahhing whenever Joe took the little dog for his daily walks. Only eight months old, Neville was full of zest and vigor. The little dog had a constant spring in his step, and curiosity would have killed him had he been a cat.

It was too bad his son didn't have a cat. Joe liked cats, and they had always had one when Zac was growing up. Cats were calm. They didn't need much of your time, and they didn't need to be walked or trained. But Nicole had wanted a dog, and the two of them loved the little guy. Hard not to, really. He was cute.

Joe would have liked it better if they had given Neville to Nicole's parents to watch, but once her parents learned Nicole would be away during the holidays, they had booked themselves on a three-month cruise. Convenient for them. Inconvenient for him. Especially when he had to get his stock ready for the late-November craft fair and complete his custom orders for Christmas.

What was he supposed to do with the

dog while he was in his studio? Neville would get in the way, and it wasn't a safe place for a dog. The dog yapped again, and Joe scowled. Then he looked down to see Neville smiling up at him, and he found himself returning the smile.

"Come on, Neville, it's time to go in. You can stay in the living room until I take you for a walk."

He thought back to his son's instructions about looking after the dog. "Don't forget: Neville likes walks at five or six at night and again at seven in the morning," Zac had said to him the night before.

"And he's crate trained," Nicole added. "We keep him in the crate during the day."

Joe took the dog into the house and unhooked the leash. "Well, Neville, I don't know why they would keep you in a crate all day. Seems mean when a dog just wants to run around." He took the dog by its collar and put him into the crate, placing a water dish inside in case he got thirsty. "I'll be back in a couple of hours to take you for your walk." The little dog whined and looked up at him through the bars.

"Don't look at me like that," Joe said. "I'll be back soon." He turned and walked outside to his studio in the backyard. The dog would be fine. Apparently, Zac and Nicole kept him contained for several hours a day while they were working.

He looked at his watch; it was three in the afternoon. He could get two hours of work in before taking Neville out. He pulled his cell phone out of his pocket, set an alarm to remind him when it was five, and put the phone on a bench just inside his studio door. He could get an order finished if he worked fast enough today.

He walked around the room to make

sure all his tools were where they should be. His former assistant, Bethany, had always been the one to gather up the tools after a project, and he missed her organizational skills. He missed having someone else in the shop with him in general, but she was now in Ontario, apprenticing in a much larger studio.

Over the next two hours, he worked on getting an important order done for a couple that had commissioned him to make an anniversary present. As he worked, he wondered if they would make it past seven years. The seven-year itch was real. He could vouch for that. That was the year Maeve had left him and Zac to fend for themselves.

He hadn't thought about Maeve since Zac's wedding, and hadn't seen her often since she left them to travel the world with a whale research ship. And now Zac was gone too, though his trip was about turtles and not whales. At least his was a dream he and Nicole shared. Maeve had never even asked Joe if he would want to go with her.

He pushed thoughts of Maeve from his mind to focus on his work. Within a few minutes, he slipped into a creative flow that lasted until he put the finishing touches on his project.

Joe was just wrapping it up when the alarm went on his telephone. *Good timing.* It would be nice to get out and stretch his legs. That was one good thing about having a dog around, at least.

When Joe turned off the alarm, he noticed a text from Zac. His son must have sent it from Vancouver. *Nic said to remind you that Neville has learned to get out of his crate, and you should put a paperclip into the latch.* Joe remembered that now. Something about wiring the door shut. It seemed a bit like overkill to him, so he had forgotten that detail as soon as she told him.

He texted back. *Thanks for the reminder. Have a wonderful trip. Text me when you get to your destination.*

A text message came back right away: *We're on the plane. Taking off in a couple minutes. I'll let you know when we get there.*

Love you, Joe texted back. *I'll talk to you soon.*

He walked down the path to the house and let himself in. The he looked around the room, trying to comprehend what was in front of him.

"Neville?" The crate was empty, and so he walked further into the house and looked around the living room. The carpet was covered in white fluff—the stuffing from the two pillows that had once graced the sofa. The cases to the pillows were shredded, and pieces of blue and gray fabric were everywhere, but he couldn't see the dog.

"Neville?" He walked cautiously around the room, peeking under the sofa and chair. What a mess. How much more damage did the little guy do? He walked into the kitchen, where a cupboard door was hanging open and a box of crackers was strewn across the slate floor. He drew his hand across his face and shook his head. Hopefully the dog had eaten nothing that would harm him. "Neville?" He walked back into the living room and paused, listening hard. A small whimper. He followed the sound toward a pile of fluff and took a closer look. It was the nose he saw first, poking out from under the chair at the far side of the room. "There you are," he said, bending down and grabbing the dog before he could wriggle free. Neville came willingly. Was he sick? What had he eaten?

The dog turned over in his arms and looked up at him, smiling his little dog smile before wriggling free and running away. He seemed okay, although Joe now knew why Nicole had warned him. He would have to take a few hours and build the dog a run behind the workshop. It would give Neville something to do other than find ways to escape.

He looked around the room again and sighed. "Let's clean this up later," he said to the dog, walking to the counter and grabbing Neville's leash. "Come on. We'll go for a walk."

Neville was there in a shot, wagging his tail and waiting.

Joe smiled at the little guy and snapped his leash onto his collar. "Let's go, you little devil."

And Neville pranced ahead of him, ready for an adventure.

CHAPTER 3

*H*elen left town directly after school to avoid rush-hour traffic and drove the two hours to Sunshine Bay, pulling into Sylvia's driveway just before six. It was a two-story home on a quiet cul-de-sac, lit up and welcoming. This was going to be a wonderful place to stay.

She climbed out of the car and walked toward the front door just as a black shape streaked out of the dark corner behind the house, nearly knocking her off-balance.

She whirled. The black cat had dashed up a nearby oak tree and was now turning to protest in the way only cats can: *Meorrw!*

Then Helen heard little footsteps on the gravel beside the house. A second streak of fur, this time white, skidded to the bottom of the tree with a high-pitched yap. *What the heck?*

The front door opened, and Sylvia hurried outside.

"Neville!" she yelled. "You get away from her!" Sylvia came to a stop in front of Helen. "Oh, I didn't see your car pull up. Welcome." She stopped and gave Helen a quick hug. "I'm sorry. I have to deal with this mess first."

She pointed toward the little Westie that was still barking at a now-hissing cat. "That is Neville, the little devil. I must take him back to Joe."

"Who's Joe?"

"The neighbor." She pointed to the

27

house next door. "I doubt he even knows the dog got out again. Joe spends a lot of time in his workshop this time of year. Here. Help me catch him."

Helen walked up behind the dog while Sylvia approached from the front. The little dog stood firmly planted, chest puffed out, laser-focused on his prey. He had a cat treed, and he wasn't giving ground to anyone. Helen liked his gumption.

"You'd think he would give the little guy more attention," she said as she approached, keeping her voice conversational so as not to startle the little guy into flight. "This breed needs a lot of exercise."

"Joe's not much of a dog person."

"Why does he have one, then?" What kind of person would have such a cute dog and not care for it properly?

"It's his son's dog, and his son is away

for a few months on a project in South America."

"And there was no one else who could watch him, I guess." The scenario made sense now, but still. Once you took on the care of an animal, you needed to follow through. She was creeping closer to Neville now, and when she was within reach, she leaned forward and grabbed his collar. The dog yelped in surprise and began to squirm, but she kept her grip tight. "Oh, no, you don't," she said to the dog. "You need to come with me." Neville squirmed some more and then yelped as she scooped him up. She held him so he was facing away from her. The last thing she needed today was to be bitten by a strange dog.

"Good show!" Sylvia said. "You did it." She then turned her attention to Angel, who was silent but still glaring at the little dog, her long black tail swishing slowly back and forth. "Now all I need to do is coax Angel out of that tree."

Helen pulled the disgruntled dog closer to her while he continued to wriggle back and forth, trying to escape. "Shh," Helen said. "I'm not going to hurt you."

As though sensing she was telling the truth, he stilled and allowed her to hold him closer.

"He seems to like you," Sylvia said.

"He's a cute little guy. Looks like he's not very old. Still trainable." The dog had gone from stiff to pliable as she held him, and now he was snuggling against her. "Let's get you home, little one," she said to him in a calm voice. "He lives just there?" she asked Sylvia, nodding her head toward the neighboring house.

"Yes. That's Joe's place. If he isn't in the house, he'll be in the back in his studio. There's fairly good lighting between the two buildings." Sylvia turned her attention to the cat up the tree. "If you get our little visitor home, I'll see what I can do about getting Angel down. Then we can have dinner."

Helen spoke to Neville as she walked down the pathway to the front door of the next house and, holding him firmly with one arm, knocked at the door. No answer. The little Westie wriggled again, and she brought her other hand around him to keep him still. "It's okay. You can get down in a few minutes. Let's get you to your person first." She took the dog around the corner of the house to the backyard, where an outbuilding stood not far away. The door to the building was ajar, and she could see light shining out into the darkness. "I think we found him," she murmured to the dog, and she walked the distance between the buildings. She knocked before entering but, hearing no answer, she pushed open the door and stepped into the warm room. It took a moment for her eyes to adjust to the bright light and a few moments longer for her to make sense of what she was seeing.

The room was lined with shelves of glassware. Bowls, glasses, swans, turtles—each item more beautiful than the one beside it. Magnificent. She wanted to browse the shelves and touch them to feel their beauty.

Across the room, a man with more gray hair than brown was facing away from her and holding a long metal rod in a blazing furnace. The dog whined, and she shushed him so as not to startle the man, who was obviously absorbed in whatever he was doing. What *was* he doing, anyway?

The dog quieted again, and she stepped closer to get a better line of sight. The man—presumably this was Joe—

stood six feet high and wore a loose-fitting T-shirt that didn't hide the toned body underneath. He was a man who either did a lot of manual labor or spent a lot of time in the gym. Her eyes drifted past his biceps, which flexed as he turned the metal tube in the furnace. She liked how his worn jeans fit over his butt. It had been many years since she had noticed a man's butt anywhere outside a movie screen. But movie-screen butts didn't count. They weren't real. Joe—now he was real. Her hand itched to reach out and touch him—just to be sure.

He stepped back and withdrew the long rod from the furnace. At the end of it, she could see a glistening vase. "Oh," she said, involuntarily. The vase was cobalt blue with swirls of white and silver shot throughout. How had he done that? He turned toward her, startled. "Oh," she said again, this time in response to his eyes.

They were molten brown, the kind that melted more than a few hearts. Appropriate, given the setting. And his eyes fit so well into his masculine face: sharp planes, high cheekbones, lips she was sure would taste so good. She licked her lips. His eyebrows were drawn together in...

Anger?

"What are you doing in here?" he boomed, startling her into loosening her grip. Neville wriggled free and jumped to the ground.

Helen looked at the man, then turned to watch the dog go.

"Wait!" she yelled as Neville galloped toward the door and disappeared outside. "Now look what you've done. I was just bringing him home." She started to go after the dog.

"Who are you?" he asked, stopping her mid-step.

"Helen," she said, before hurrying out the door.

~

"Helen," Joe whispered as he watched the green-eyed goddess who had invaded his studio run out into the night. It was a suitable name for a goddess. Particularly one with flaming auburn hair. He should go after her, try to catch the little dog, but that would mean stopping work on the vase, and it was nearly done. If he stopped now, he would lose momentum on the project, and he needed to get it done today. He had promised the couple that their vase would ready for their latest viewing the next afternoon.

He worked as quickly as he could, his focus divided between the glass and what was going on outside. How had the dog managed to get out of the run he had built? He thought it was Neville-proofed for sure this time, but apparently not.

The vase was turning out well, and he hoped it would meet with their approval. He could tell it was important to the couple. Their tradition was to incorporate wedding colours into their anniversary gift to each other. For their second anniversary the year before, they had commissioned a blue-and-white quilt made of cotton. This year, according to tradition, they would mark the occasion with glass or crystal. Joe scowled at the sentimentality of it all, but who was he to argue when he was getting paid?

The glass was finally shaped the way he had envisioned, and he set it in the annealer to slowly cool. He put away his tools for the day and went outside, switching off the light and turning to lock the door.

The moon wasn't bright tonight, but the floodlights from his security system lit up the backyard. Still, he walked carefully to avoid any holes Neville had dug. It had been two weeks, and Joe was filling the holes as fast as he found them, but he'd discovered another one that morning when he went out to mulch the vegetable beds and get them ready for winter. He walked to the other side of the shop, where he had built the dog run, and took Neville's leash from the hook. He would need this if he were going to bring him home. Now, where to start?

"Neville?" he called out.

"Over here," Helen said from the far corner of the yard. "Oh, ouch!"

What had that dog done now? "Hello?" he said, walking toward her voice. "Are you okay?"

"I'm fine," she said. "I just turned my

foot a little. You have holes all over this yard, you know."

"Damn dog," he said under his breath, quickening his step as much as he dared. Who knew where Neville had dug in the past couple of hours before escaping the yard? He could see Helen now, crouched. She was looking at Neville, who had scuttled back against the fence, whining in protest. Hopefully he hadn't already dug an escape hatch under that section of the fence.

Helen stood when Joe got closer. "I can't get him to come. He's afraid of me now. I thought we'd become friends."

She looked disappointed, and Joe had a sudden urge to hug her close and assure her it wasn't personal. Instead he said, "Neville has a mind of his own. I think Zac, my son, was trying to train him before he left, but none of the lessons seem to have set in yet."

"Usually it has more to do with the trainer than the dog," she countered, but she seemed to think better of what she had said. "I don't mean to say your son didn't try. I mean, I've never even met him."

"Zac only got the dog two months ago, and then he found out about the opportunity in Nicaragua. I don't think Neville even had three lessons. Once my busy season is over, I'll take him to obedience school."

"And until then?"

"I take him for walks and try to tire him out. I also built him a run... that he seems to have escaped from. I'll have to produce another solution for tomorrow. I have a craft fair next week I need to get ready for."

"There's always puppy daycare," she said.

Puppy daycare. Why hadn't he

thought of that? It would be expensive, but if he didn't get the dog under control, he would never make his deadlines. "That's a good idea. I'll look into that."

She smiled up at him as though he had just told her she'd won a million dollars. He could look at that smile all day long. Then he remembered the last auburn-haired goddess who had looked at him like that, and he frowned. That hadn't ended well.

"First, I have to catch him," he said, to cover his sudden mood change. It wasn't Helen's fault she looked like Maeve, and it wasn't Helen's fault Maeve had left him for whale watching and her ex-boyfriend.

"He might come to you," she said.

"Maybe. Let's see." He crept slowly toward Neville, speaking to him as calmly as he could, trying to keep his anger from seeping out. He had been trying to build rapport with this dog for two weeks, and he had thought he was making a breakthrough. Neville watched him approach, and his whining soon became whimpers. Then the dog came toward him, head lowered in submission, presenting his collar so Joe could clip the leash on. "Good dog," Joe said. "Let's go get you some dinner."

"Oh, good," Helen said, following along beside them. "I was beginning to think I would be here all night." They walked back to the front of the house, and he stopped outside the front door. She stooped to pat Neville on the head, and the dog wagged his tail so hard his entire body shook.

"It looks like he's your friend again," said Joe, looking down at her. She stood and gazed at him with those bewitching eyes. Green like new grass shot with gold flecks. He didn't want to blink. Then he heard a growl, different this time than

Neville's, and Helen blushed in embarrassment.

"Sorry, I haven't had dinner yet. I should go." Her stomach growled again, as though it agreed with her. But she didn't move—she just stood, looking up at him.

"Thanks for bringing him back," he said, trying to prolong the conversation just a little.

"Not a problem. But they will be holding dinner for me. I should go." It wasn't until she had walked down the path—and out of his life—that he realized he had no idea who she was or where she had found Neville. He heard a small whine and looked down at the dog, who was looking off into the distance.

"I know, boy. I liked her too," he said. "But she has people waiting for her already. Let's go. Time to eat."

On the street, Helen paused a moment and looked back toward the house she had just left. Had she just imagined that? Or had he seemed as attracted to her as she was to him? If not for the dog and her growling stomach, she might have stayed to see where that went. But he was Sylvia's neighbor, and she didn't want to embarrass herself by hitting on him. Besides, he probably looked at all women that way. Intensely. With those beautiful dark eyes. As though he wanted to devour them. Her stomach growled again. It prompted her to put thoughts of Joe away for now and get back to Sylvia's place.

As she walked down the driveway, Helen looked up at the tree in the front yard and was pleased to see it no longer held a cat. *Good.* With luck, the rest of the evening would hold less drama. It had been a long day. Teaching, driving, and dog catching was hard work. She was looking forward to one of Sylvia's home-cooked meals and a glass of wine.

She walked to her car, relieved to find her purse still on the floor of the passenger's side. Thankfully, she was in Sunshine Bay rather than somewhere her purse might have "walked off." She grabbed her overnight bag and the bottle of wine she had brought, then climbed the steps of the porch.

Sylvia flung the door open before Helen could knock. "Finally! I was just going to send Jack out to find you." She took the bottle of wine from Helen's outstretched hand. "Oh, thank you. This will go well with dinner." She opened the door wider and stepped back. "Come in. Jack! Helen's back. We can stand down on the search."

Jack, a white-haired gentleman who

always reminded Helen of a thinner version of Santa Claus, stepped into the hall.

"Did Neville get away again?" he asked.

"How did you know?"

Sylvia laughed. "That dog is an escape artist. Jack, can you show Helen her room and where to set down her things, please?" Then she turned to Helen. "Then come right back. Dinner is ready."

Helen followed Jack upstairs to the spare bedroom and placed her luggage inside the door. It was a comfortable room, all grays and whites, with a big four-poster that looked as soft as a feather bed.

She used the ensuite, which was just as welcoming as the bedroom, right down to the scented candles, the potpourri in a crystal bowl, and the big fluffy towels. It had been a good idea to come here this weekend. It was like coming home to a place where she was safe and wanted, and it had been a long time since she'd felt people wanted to be in her company.

Helen quickly returned to the kitchen helped Sylvia carry the food out to the table. Angel, the cat, was curled up on the seat of the big bay window at the front of the room, purring loudly. Content.

"She looks no worse for her ordeal with Neville," Helen said, nodding toward the cat.

"She's getting used to Neville, I think. The tree is her favorite escape route. He can't get her, and she knows I will rescue her quickly. I do wish that Joe had someone to help him. I know how busy he is this time of year."

"He makes beautiful things, doesn't he?" Helen said. "The studio rather stunned me. I was expecting some old woodworking shop or something."

"You're lucky to get a chance to see his studio this time of year. Usually he does open houses when he has some help, but lately he's been working a lot more on his own."

"Bethany is away at school this year," Jack said.

"Bethany?" Helen asked.

"Bethany worked with Joe for the past two or three summers. This year she started attending college for glassblowing in Ontario. She'll be back for Christmas, but I don't think that includes helping Joe," said Jack.

"He should probably put Neville into a day care for the rest of his busy season," Sylvia said. "That dog needs a lot more attention than he's getting."

"He is a cute little guy, though." Helen thought of how the little dog had smiled up at her when she left him behind with Joe. *A cute big guy, too*, she mused.

But not for her. The last thing she wanted was to get involved with her friend's neighbor, especially one who wasn't a dog person.

While they ate, they caught up on what had been happening in each other's lives. When they were done, Jack made excuses to go and watch a show, and the two women made their way to the kitchen to clean up. "How are you *really* doing?" Sylvia asked as she handed Helen a plate to dry. "I know this past year hasn't been easy for you."

"I'm looking forward to coming here for Christmas. Ever since you asked me, the idea has been growing on me. It will allow me to explore the town and meet a few people. I have wonderful memories of my time here."

"I just wish you could come a little sooner," said Sylvia. "Jack wants to get in a visit with his cousin and tour some places he used to visit growing up." She paused and looked down at her feet. "Oh, hello. Are you ready for your dinner?" Angel was rubbing against Sylvia's leg, tail held high.

Helen bent down to pet the cat, and Angel moved away.

"It takes her time to warm up to people. But she didn't bolt, so it looks like she likes you," Sylvia said. She opened a can of cat food. "Come on, then," she said to Angel as she dumped the contents of the tin into a dish beside the counter. The cat walked over for her supper. "I'm glad she hasn't taken an instant dislike to you. It makes it easier to leave."

Helen took her turn at the sink to wash the next cup. "How soon did you want to leave? My contract ends two weeks before Christmas. The woman I've been filling in for is returning part-time beginning next week, so I'll have time to wrap up some things at home. I could come earlier."

"Really?" Sylvia grinned. "That would be wonderful. Jack has been really looking forward to the trip to the Okanagan, and since we want to visit as many people as possible, he'd hoped to leave on the sixteenth of December. Of course, I'll need to find someone to take over my volunteer jobs if I'm going to do that." She was talking to herself now, Helen mused. Maybe she could help— and explore this town even further at the same time. Get on the teacher's on-call list. Look at some properties. *Don't get ahead of yourself,* she thought, but meeting people would be a start.

"Maybe I could do some of your volunteer jobs for you," she said.

Sylvia turned toward her in surprise "I hadn't thought of that, but that would be the perfect solution. It would give you something to do while you're here, introduce you to some new people, and give you a deeper impression of our small town."

"Like a test-drive with no obligation to purchase," Helen said. "What kind of jobs have you committed to?" More to the point, what was she getting herself into?

"The Tree Festival and Auction on Christmas Eve. It's more like an indoor family fair. Lots of things for the kids to do, and an auction of trees full of Christmas ornaments—the ornaments, not the trees. Each tree is sponsored by a company in town and auctioned off at the end of the evening. It's a fundraiser for the hospital. The following day, there's a Community Winter Feast. It's a great time. We have a buffet that serves a traditional Christmas dinner but with other options—everything from biriyani to vegan fare. A little something for everyone. I've agreed to help source the food and organize the volunteers. Normally I would also stay and decorate, help cook the dinner, and sometimes we even attend. It's always a lot of fun. There are singalongs, a performance by the local drama club, a reading of one of Dickens's tales, and other stories from around the world. All kinds of things." Her eyes were alight, and Helen couldn't help but feel her excitement.

"Sounds like a lot of fun."

"And not that much time, really. A few hours a week to start. A few days before the events, there is more of a commitment, but it's a talented group of volunteers. What do you think?"

"I think it sounds perfect," Helen said. It would give her something to do during the holiday season, and helping others was the best way she knew to ease the loneliness.

Sylvia wiped her hands on the dishtowel and set it aside. "I can't wait to tell Jack. He's going to be so happy he'll burst."

Helen put the last few dishes away and put the kettle on for tea. It would be good to spend some more time here, to find out if the town would suit as her new home.

And it would get her away from Sam and Jillian. She really couldn't face another year of seeing them together while she sat next door alone. She thought of the unopened manila envelope upstairs in her luggage. Maybe soon she could finally let go of their marriage.

Sam already had.

CHAPTER 4

*H*elen worked part-time for the rest of November and filled the rest of her time tackling the last two rooms she hadn't got to over the summer break.

It took more time and energy than she thought it would. Each bauble and piece of clothing, old lamp and ornament held a memory of better times—or at least times she thought had been better. Sam was a part of everything, and though it was hard to let those things go, it was hardest to let go of the things from when Kim was small.

They had been happy then. Or so she had thought. Even when Sam had been away on conferences or courses for his job as financial advisor, she had loved those years. That was when Jill had come into her life, and the two of them did everything together: raised their children and shared secrets, dreams, fears, and joys.

It was harder than she'd anticipated to sift through the reminders of Jillian: the knitting from a class Jill had wanted to take, the paintings and the stained-glass lamp from classes Helen had dragged Jill to. Jill was like the sister she'd never had, and she had lost her. She had lost her entire family in the space of a few months.

There was a knock at the door, and she opened it to find Jill on her doorstep.

"What are you doing here?" She

wanted to yell and scream and throw things, but instead, she counted backward in her head, trying to stay calm.

"I came to talk to you," Jill said. "I wanted to... explain."

"Jill, it's too late to explain. You stole my life."

"You never really liked your life, though. You used to tell me how much he ignored you. How mismatched you were. How you'd grown apart."

"But why did it have to be *you* who took him? I trusted you. I loved you like a sister."

"I loved you too. I never meant to hurt you. I... You can't help who you fall in love with, Helen. I..."

"I think you'd better go." Helen started to close the door, cursing Jill in her head. How had she trusted this woman? How could she not have known?

"You know you don't love him

anymore," Jill said, putting her foot in the door and forcing her way in. "Sign the papers. Let him go."

"Get out of here, Jill."

"Why don't you just start over? Sell the house. It's too big for you anyway now that Kim's gone."

"You want me to just sneak off into the sunset?"

"No," Jill said. "I'm not saying this right. It's just that you always wanted more. Maybe it's time for you to travel or paint or... do all those things Sam never wanted to do."

"Jill, why are you here?"

"He's asked me to marry him," she said. "I don't want to hurt you, but... for the sake of our friendship, all those years together..."

"Get out." Helen felt stone cold inside. Here was her former best friend, who knew all her secrets, trying to use those secrets against her.

"Please, Helen. You know you don't want him." Jill stepped backward to the porch.

"Get out of my house!" Helen said. "And if you know what's good for you, you won't come back."

Jill looked as though Helen has struck her. She backed up and made her way down the steps of the front porch. "I am sorry about how this all happened," Jill said. "But it's time..."

Helen slammed the door on her former friend and went back to the room she was clearing out with a different lens. Every single item that represented something she and her former friend had done together was soon in a large bin that she took to the backyard. She needed fire for this. Fire to burn away the old sadness. Maybe then she could let him go. She ignited the first thing, one of her first attempts at an oil painting, and fed it into the burn barrel, and then piece after piece of their shared life went into the flames.

As she watched the flames grow stronger, she thought of Joe in front of the furnace, creating something beautiful out of molten glass. That's what she needed to do. Make a new life out of the ashes. Not that she wanted to replace Sam with another man the way Jill had with her own husband. She wanted to let go of her past and move on—but not because Jill asked her to, and not on Jill's timetable. She would sign those papers when she was good and ready, and not before.

CHAPTER 5

Three weeks later, Helen locked up her house for the second time in a month and drove to Sunshine Bay. When she pulled into Sylvia's driveway, she looked at the nearby tree and was disappointed not to find Neville there, barking, though she was afraid to examine the reason. Nor did she want to examine why, the past few nights, she'd been having dreams that made her awaken drenched in sweat—and not the kind that came from a hot flash.

Sylvia met her at the door and helped her take her bags to her room. "I'm so glad you're here," Sylvia said. "I've invited the Tree Festival committee over to introduce you. They'll be here right after dinner."

"Throwing me in at the deep end?" she said, setting her luggage down.

"It's not like you aren't a strong swimmer already," Sylvia laughed. "If you can wrangle preteens swimming in hormone soup, you can do this."

"I suppose you have a point."

Helen listened while Sylvia showed her where she could keep her things. Half a closet and two empty drawers were cleared out and set aside for her. That feeling of being wanted was creeping in again, and it felt so good.

They had an early dinner, and Sylvia set out dessert squares and sugar cookies on a plate while Helen made the tea and coffee for the expected guests.

The first to arrive was Estelle, who reminded Helen of a kindly matron. She kept her white hair drawn into a bun and wore a smart sweater set and pressed slacks. She gave the impression of someone who was in charge, and it wasn't a surprise to learn that she was the committee chair.

The next two, Michelle and Lydia, arrived together. Michelle had short, dark hair and wore leggings and a T-shirt. She was a yoga instructor with a class to teach at seven thirty. The gym was just down the road, and she gave Helen her card. "Maybe you'd like to sign up for some lessons while you're here. If you give them my card, you can get ten percent off your first ten."

"Always the salesperson," Sylvia laughed, and Michelle smiled. "And we appreciate your skills when it comes to ticket sales, don't we, Lydia?"

Lydia, a slim woman who looked to be in her late thirties or early forties, chuckled. "Indeed." She reached out to Helen. "I'm the treasurer for the committee. Welcome, and thank you for agreeing to take up some of Sylvia's tasks. She'll be missed."

"Thanks for letting me help," Helen said. "I hope I can be of some use in her absence. I've worked on some projects with Sylvia in the past when we both ended up on teacher committees together. She's a powerhouse."

Sylvia waved away the compliment and went to answer the doorbell.

"Sorry I'm late," said a familiar male voice from the doorway.

"It's okay," said Sylvia. "We're just settling in." Everyone turned toward the newcomer as he stepped into the room. "Joe, I think you met my friend Helen Baker the last time she was here. She's going to be cat-sitting for Angel this month, and she's agreed to take on my tasks while Jack and I are away."

Helen sat, dumbstruck. If she had thought he looked good in the dark and in her dreams, she had been very much mistaken. In full light and cleaned up, the man was beautiful. And now she was on a committee where she would have to work more closely with him.

This trip was getting better and better.

*J*oe was momentarily silenced by the sight of the woman he had been unable to stop thinking about in weeks. She had disappeared into the night, and now, just when he had decided she was a creation of his imagination, here she was. Next door. In Sylvia and Jack's house.

"Can I take your coat?" Sylvia asked.

"Yes, of course." He fumbled with the coat buttons, slipped it off, and handed it to Sylvia, who had an amused look on her face. "Welcome to Sunshine Bay, Helen," he said, approaching the room.

"Oh, you can sit here," Lydia said, scooting over so he could squeeze in. He looked at her and at the place beside her, and then he searched the room for other chairs. They were all taken. His fault for being late, he supposed, though in truth it was Neville's fault. The little devil had run away when Joe tried to get his leash on for a walk. Neville always wanted to play when it was least convenient.

"Thanks," he murmured, settling onto the sofa beside Lydia, their thighs touching from lack of space. He hadn't known Lydia long, but she had a knack for saving him seats, joining him on the same work duties, and being physically close to him. It was disconcerting. She was a nice-looking woman—long dark hair, fit from working out at her friend's yoga studio— and she was kind, and a good addition to any committee, but there wasn't a spark there. He was at a loss at how to tell her he wasn't interested without hurting her. So he had always just ignored her advances. Now, however, Helen was watching him with doubt on her face. But her expression changed to surprise when Angel the cat jumped up on his lap.

To defuse the situation, he laughed.

"Well, hello there." The cat kneaded her paws into his leg, settled on his lap, and purred.

"I'm not sure I should leave," Sylvia said. "Angel will forget I even exist with you and Helen around."

A tinkle of laughter came from the other side of the room, and Helen said, "No chance of that. She knows who feeds her."

He liked Helen's laughter. It was infectious, and so was her smile. He liked everything he knew about her so far. Including the fact that she was just visiting. If he asked her out for dinner or a coffee, there would be no fear of a long-term commitment. And when she left again, there would be no hard feelings. A perfect relationship, really. The only kind he'd ever indulged in since his divorce.

"When are you and Jack leaving town, Sylvia?" he asked. If she left soon, it would be only neighborly for him to show Helen around town.

"First thing in the morning," said Sylvia. "As soon as we've got Helen settled."

"Well, Helen." He turned toward her. "If there's anything you need when Jack and Sylvia are away, please don't hesitate to call. Sylvia has my number."

"Yes, I'll make sure you have it before I leave," Sylvia said to Helen. But she was looking straight at Joe when she said it. "Knowing how often Neville ends up over here, you might need it."

"Who's Neville?" Lydia asked.

Helen laughed again. "Neville is Joe's dog, and he has a habit of being absent from home without leave." She turned to Joe, and he couldn't help but smile back. "Did you get his run patched okay?"

"I did, and I've taken your advice and

sent him to day care for the last two weeks. He is exhausted when he gets home, but unfortunately, I'll need a plan B for the next few weeks. The day care is all booked with dogs boarding over the holiday."

"Well, if there's anything I can do to help you with Neville, I'd be glad to," said Helen. "He's a cute little thing."

"What kind of dog is he?" Lydia asked, and Joe reluctantly turned away from Helen to answer her.

"A Westie. He's actually my son's dog."

"I didn't know you had a son," Lydia said. "Which school does he go to?"

"My son's thirty. He lives in Vancouver. And right now, he's on a trip to Nicaragua with his wife." Maybe if she understood how old his son was, she'd lose interest.

Lydia's eyes widened, and her mouth

form an O of surprise. *Good.* His comment had hit the mark.

"You don't look old enough to have a thirty-year-old," Lydia blurted. He had miscalculated the impact of his son's age. It wasn't the first time a woman had said that to him—as if flattery would somehow erase their age gap.

"Well, I feel it sometimes," he said.

"How long has he lived away from home?" Helen asked.

"Ten years. Though it feels like just yesterday when he was here."

"I know what you mean. My daughter left home five years ago to go to university in Vancouver, and then this summer she married and moved out east to Toronto. I miss her every day."

"So she's—what? Twenty-three or so?"

"Yes. A little young for marriage, but they are great together."

Michelle interrupted them. "Listen, I

have a class to teach this evening. Is there something specific we need to discuss tonight?"

Estelle took her cue and called the meeting to order. They spent the next forty minutes dividing up the tasks. Lydia and Michelle left right after the meeting to make it to their yoga class, and Joe got up to leave as well. He had to get the rest of the ornaments done for the tree he was sponsoring this year, but he didn't want Estelle to know he was behind.

"Joe," Estelle said, "I want you to take Helen under your wing since you live right next door. Can you see that she knows where to go and how to get there for the Tree Festival? It's going to be a lot of work over the next two weeks to get the festival and dinner ready."

Joe turned to Helen, who looked like she was holding her breath. "Absolutely," he said. "You can count on me." And he was rewarded with the sunniest smile he had seen in a very long time.

As he was leaving, Helen came up to him and said, "I was serious, you know. If you need someone to take Neville for a walk in the mornings, let me know. It would give me something to do."

"You're serious? He has to walk at seven in the morning."

"I get up early all the time. I could start tomorrow if you like. Sylvia and Jack are getting the first ferry, so they'll be gone by then."

"Okay, I'll see you tomorrow. I'll have the coffee on."

Joe wanted to click his heels as he walked home. He spent the next hour clearing up the clutter in the living room and wiping down the kitchen. If she was coming into his house for coffee, he didn't want to scare her off.

CHAPTER 6

Sylvia and Jack left before dawn, leaving Helen and Angel alone for the first time. Helen went to the kitchen to fill Angel's food and water dishes and then turned to the cat.

"Well, what are you doing today?"

Angel blinked slowly, walked into the living room, curled up the window seat, and closed her eyes.

"Well, then. Since your plans don't include me, I'm going out for a walk."

She put on her winter things and walking shoes, locked up the door behind her, and walked quickly to Joe's house. Neville's walks were at seven, so she wanted to get there on time.

Her heart was pounding by the time she got next door—not from the brisk walk, but from the anticipation of seeing Joe. She had woken in damp sheets again, flooded with dream memories of heat and skin and lips and... She tamped down her visions. The last thing Joe needed when he opened the door was a woman who looked ready to jump him.

He probably wasn't even interested in a woman his own age when he had young women like Lydia wanting him. She thought back to the evening before and tried to see what she hadn't seen with Sam and Jillian—an attraction blooming right under her nose.

She stepped up to his front door and

knocked, banishing thoughts of Jill and Sam until later. Much later. Right now, she just wanted to see Neville and take him for a walk. He, at least, could always be trusted to be truthful and up front. Dogs were honest and always happy to see you, no matter what.

The door opened, and Joe was there in a T-shirt very much like the one she'd removed in her dream the night before. Her skin warmed from the blush that overtook her whole body, and she quickly refocused on the dog that was vying for her attention with small whines and a wagging tail.

"Good morning," she said, glancing at Joe and then bending down to pat the little dog. "Are you ready for your walk?"

"Would you like to start with a cup of coffee? I just finished brewing a pot." His deep voice was soothing, and she waited for her blush to recede before standing again.

"That would be great. I had a cup with Sylvia and Jack about an hour ago, but I could go for another one now that I'm awake." It would give her a chance to talk to him without thirty-five-year-olds draped all over him—a chance to see if her attraction was, or could be, reciprocated.

"I have some blueberry muffins, too, if you want one. I got them from the bakery yesterday."

"That sounds fantastic. I haven't had breakfast yet." She rarely ate breakfast when she wasn't working, but today she would make an exception.

They sat at the table, and she took a sip of the coffee. "This is good."

"I get it from a little bistro just a few blocks away. The Beehive roasts their own ethical beans, so I like to support them."

"I'll have to try it out. I'm always looking for a good cup of coffee."

Neville danced around their feet, perhaps thinking he would get a scrap or two of whatever the humans were eating. "I don't think you'll like these," Joe said to him. "You should go check out the food in your dish over there."

"Neville. Off," said Helen. "May I try something?" she asked Joe. "Do you have any dog treats for him?"

"Sure." He shrugged. "Over there in the cupboard above the counter."

She got the treats, placing a few in her pocket for later, and then showed a treat to Neville. "Look at me," she said, and the little dog looked up and received a treat. "Look at me." Again, he was rewarded for looking up.

"Okay, good start. Now. Look at me again." She took the treat and placed it in his dog dish. "There you go. Eat your breakfast."

Neville walked over to the dish and ate the food, and Helen returned to the table to have her coffee.

"Where'd you learn that?"

"I had a dog when I was a kid."

"What do you do when he comes back to beg at the table?"

"Ignore him. If you reward him, he'll continue to beg. When he's not begging, you reward him by asking him to do something else. He has to know you're the one in charge."

"I'll give that a try. Thanks for the tip."

"Not a problem. If it's okay, I'll try to teach him to heel when we're out on our walks."

"Absolutely, if you promise to show me how it's done." He put a muffin on a plate and placed it in front of her. "Butter?"

"No, thanks. This looks great just the way it is."

"Do you have any animals now?"

"No. I had a cat, but it was my husband's. He took it with him when he left."

"How long ago did he leave?" He looked directly into her eyes as he asked, as though perhaps he was asking something else.

She gazed back at him until the connection became too intimate. She looked down at her plate and tore off a piece of muffin.

"A year."

"I'm sorry."

She looked up, and he did genuinely look sorry. Sorrier, in fact, than a lot of her former friends had looked when they'd said the same words. She couldn't help but wonder, yet again, how many people had known about the affair and how long it had been going on.

"Well, there's nothing to be done about it. He's not coming back." Her voice softened as she tried to contain the emotion that crept in whenever she thought about the betrayal. She didn't want her anger and hurt to get between her and anyone in Sunshine Bay, especially Joe. "How about you? Is there a woman in your life?"

She had to ask. Maybe, if she had asked Sam more direct questions instead of pussyfooting around and assuming things were okay, she would have figured it all out sooner.

"No. My wife left me... us... my son and I... when Zac was six. She went back to working on a research ship—and back to a man she had known before she knew me."

"Oh." She placed her hand on his arm. "I'm sorry. That must have been hard."

He looked down at her hand, but he didn't move his arm. Then he placed his other hand over hers. "Thanks. It was a long time ago, and it took me years to forgive her, but it's the right life for her. She would have hated living here in Sunshine Bay. While I think it's a paradise, she thought it was a cage. And motherhood, at least that traditional kind, wasn't for her. She took Zac every summer for a month, though, and they've stayed connected over the years through satellite phone, computer chats, and such." His eyes glazed over as though he were remembering something from long ago. It was obvious he had once loved his wife. Maybe he still did.

"And you never felt the need to marry again?"

He sat back, removing his hands to his lap and breaking their tenuous connection. "No. I've had a few flings over the years, but nothing serious. I had Zac. He was my main person. And I had my work." He glanced over her shoulder at the clock. "Speaking of which, I need to get back to it. I have a few more ornaments to make for this year's tree."

"You make ornaments for the tree festival?"

"Every year. The money goes to support the hospital. When my father was sick, I spent a lot of time there. It's a way to give back."

"That's a nice tradition."

"Zac used to help me with the fused glass ornaments when he was younger, though he never got much into it. All his ornaments looked like turtles." He laughed, and she watched his eyes light up.

"He likes turtles?"

"Yes. He takes after his mother that way. He and his wife left to go on a research trip this year."

Was his voice breaking? No. It was probably just an early-morning frog in his throat. As if in answer to her unspoken question, he cleared his throat. "Which is why I have Neville." He glanced at the clock again. "I really do need to get to the workshop."

"Right, yes. And Neville is probably eager to get his walk in." She stood and put her plate and cup in the sink. "Where's his leash?"

Moments later, they were out on the porch.

"I'll take him for about an hour if that's okay. Where should I put him when I get back? I don't want to disturb your work."

He motioned for her to follow him

around to the back of the house. "See the run? I usually put him in there. There's a hatch at the back. I put in that little shelter so he has a place to go when it gets colder. It stays pretty warm. Anyway, just make sure you latch it up well. He's a smart little guy."

She glanced back up at him, but his eyes were on the workshop. He definitely had a one- track mind.

"Which is the best way to go for a good walk?" she asked, standing back.

"Go left if you want to walk down to the shops. Go right if you want to go to the park."

"Thanks," she said. "Want to go to town, Neville? Let's see what there is in the windows." And soon the little dog was leading the way out of the yard and down the street, happy to stop and wag his tail at every passerby they came across. Maybe she should get a dog. It was nice to have another being to talk to.

She thought back to the conversation with Joe. She hadn't been attracted to another man in years, but he obviously wasn't over his ex-wife. And the last thing she needed was to get involved with another man who saw her as second best.

It hurt too much.

CHAPTER 7

Joe paused as he entered his studio to look over his shoulder and watch Helen and Neville walk away. Why had he shared so much with her? He hadn't talked about Maeve in years except to say he was divorced when someone asked. Her leaving had been hard—of course it had—but once she was gone and he had figured out how to juggle his work and Zac's needs, it got better. Maeve had taken her anger and resentment with her, leaving them to get on with their lives.

So what had triggered his emotion? Missing Zac? That was part of it, but it had more to do with the memory of Maeve going back to her ex-husband, Pierre. It was clear that Helen still had feelings for her husband, and he couldn't live through that brand of hurt again. He was attracted to Helen, but he needed to keep her at a distance. He needed to nip this in the bud so he didn't repeat his experience with Maeve.

Best to keep her in the same category as the other women he worked with on committees. Friend and colleague and nothing more.

He turned his mind to his work and spent the rest of the morning producing as many tree ornaments as possible. He was behind on this project and would have to complete at least four or five a day for the next couple of weeks. Bethany had taken the lead on designing the decorations in prior years, and this year she had sent a new design, *Crystal Rhapsody*. She had created it for a school project. But he would have a tough time getting the fused-glass aspects completed on time. What he really needed was a second set of hands.

He could do the blown-glass parts fairly quickly, so he started with them, grateful that her design called for plain red and plain green globes with gold running through them. The rest of the series—flat discs with pictures of drums and pipes and musical notes—would take more time. He was proud that Bethany was developing her craft— her skill destined her for a larger, more prestigious studio—but he was also sad. She'd be leaving town for good.

If he could do justice to her design, he

thought that *Crystal Rhapsody* could bring a good sum for the hospital. He just needed to push himself to make the deadline. The work went quickly, and he produced several globes before lunch, thankful that the glass he was working with was red rather than blue. The couple who had commissioned the glass vase had finally accepted his fourth attempt, and even though they had paid well, he pitied the person who had to sell them appliances—the modern gift for a fourth wedding anniversary—next year.

He went out to get Neville for a short walk before lunch. The dog was there, curled up in the little shelter at the end of the run, and he sprang to life when he saw Joe running to greet him. Joe laughed. The little guy was growing on him. Dogs weren't so bad after all.

CHAPTER 8

Helen dropped Neville off after their long, rambling walk and went home to check on Angel. The cat was still asleep on the window seat, as though she hadn't moved an inch. She opened one eye when Helen approached, and closed it again.

"You really don't talk much, do you?" said Helen. She went into the kitchen to see about food. Sylvia had left the fridge well stocked, but Helen could see a few things she needed—like eggnog, and perhaps a bit of rum to go with it. Just because she wasn't cooking a Christmas dinner this year didn't mean she had to give up all her traditions. Though she was going to have to make new ones.

She sighed. Change could be exhausting. But now that she had finished her year of firsts, letting go and grieving what she'd lost, it was time to consider another year of firsts. A year of new beginnings, a year when she could try new things, meet new people, make new friends, and...

She was getting ahead of herself. Perhaps one day she could have a new love, but she would have to meet someone first. And if she believed the women she'd met through her chat line for divorced women, it was hard to meet someone after fifty. Men that age wanted thirty-year-olds, and she had no idea who would want a fifty-six-year old. She plugged in the kettle for tea and thought of her conversation with Joe earlier that morning.

She had wondered why he was still single, but after hearing him talk about his ex-wife, she could understand. He was still obviously in love with the woman. Right now, she needed to focus on more important things than men—like what she was going to have for lunch.

Helen opened the fridge again, but it was too quiet in the house. She had to get out for a bit. What was that restaurant Joe had mentioned? She opened the map on her phone and typed in *restaurants near me*. There it was. The Beehive Bistro. She would go there. She unplugged the kettle and went to grab her coat and keys.

She arrived at the restaurant just after eleven. It was early for lunch, but she'd risen at dawn to see Sylvia and Jack on their way, eaten only a muffin for breakfast, and walked Neville for more than the original hour because she'd got lost. She was hungry.

She entered the restaurant and was pleased to find the room decorated in honey-colored wood with a stone fireplace at one end. Looking around for a place to sit, she saw Lydia, her committee partner, waving at her.

"Would you like to join me?" Lydia asked. "My friend just called to say she had an emergency. She's a doctor. It happens." She shrugged.

"Yes, that would be nice." Helen sat in the empty chair, and Lydia handed her the menu.

"I haven't ordered yet, but I would recommend the salmon salad if you're interested in lunch. Or, if you are vegetarian, there are several other great options." The server approached just then to take their orders, and along with the recommended salmon salad, Helen ordered a latte.

"So what brings you to Sunshine Bay?" Lydia asked as they sipped their drinks and waited for their meals.

"I'm doing Sylvia a favor, mostly. She's been helping me out a lot this past year, and one good turn deserves another, they say."

"Will your family be joining you for the holidays?"

This was feeling like the Spanish Inquisition, but how else did one get to know new people? "No, my daughter's spending the holidays with her husband's family this year, so there's just me. How about you?"

"There's just me and my son for the holidays this year," Lydia said. "That's why I wanted to help with the Community Winter Feast. If I can't have it with my family, I may as well help others have a good holiday season."

"Beats crying alone in your eggnog at home," Helen said, lifting her drink to take another sip.

"Exactly," Lydia laughed.

"You don't have family nearby?"

"I do, but my parents left for Arizona early this year. One of my mother's aunts had hip surgery, so she's going down to help. I could have gone to my brother's place, I suppose, but it's a long trip, and I didn't feel like driving all the way up to Kelowna this year. When Sylvia asked me to be on the committee, I thought it would be an opportunity to meet new people. I've lost a few friends since my husband died."

"Oh, I'm sorry. Was it recent?"

"Yes. Two years ago next month. Meningitis. You always think of that affecting children, but I guess you never know." Her eyes were filling with tears, and she quickly brushed them away with the napkin on her knee. She smiled brightly, as though willing them to go away. "Anyway, it was hard enough to lose my husband, but then I lost my friends too. They were married, and I guess I was some kind of threat."

"I've had the same experience since my separation."

"You have? I'm glad it's not just me. What do they think I'll do? Steal their husbands?" She laughed, and Helen smiled tightly at the unintended hit to her solar plexus. "I mean, don't get me wrong. I'm lonely, sure. But most of their husbands aren't my type anyway. And even if they were, well. I'm not lonely enough to do that to a friend."

Helen wished Jill had that attitude. Perhaps that was the other reason she was so upset with what had happened. She had stuck by Jill when her husband was sick. She had helped her out. She'd even sent Sam over to help her with things like a plugged sink, and to give her advice when her sump pump stopped working one day. Helen had to move this conversation in another direction before she cried or screamed.

"Do you work at the hospital too?" she asked, thinking of Lydia's doctor friend.

"Oh, no. I'm a dental hygienist. It's a good job. Pays well. And I can pick my hours here in town. There aren't many of us here, so I can work around Shane's schedule. How about you?"

"I'm a teacher. Well, a retired teacher, but I still work as a substitute. Which reminds me: I'll have to connect with the school board this week."

"Does that mean you're moving here?" Lydia's face lit up.

"I'm considering it. My divorce is

almost final." At least it would be if she signed the papers. "Once that's done, I'll have to sell my house as part of the settlement and move somewhere. I just haven't figured out where to go yet."

"Where do you live now?"

"Duncan."

"It's a nice little town. You can't stay there?"

"No. It's become, shall we say, uncomfortable."

Lydia raised her eyebrows. "Don't worry, you don't have to tell me anything if you don't want to talk about it." Then she added, "But if you want to talk, I'm a good listener."

"Well, ironically enough, my best friend's husband died three years ago, and she took up with my husband."

"You're kidding!" The shock on Lydia's face made Helen bark with laughter.

"I thought it was just a thing people feared," said Lydia. "I never heard of it actually happening before."

"Maybe those married friends of ours do have something to worry about," Helen said. "You know, I'm now considered the single, desperate one, and I'm shunned by all our coupled friends. Jill, my former friend, has replaced me there too."

"I'm so sorry."

Helen laughed. "Don't worry about it. It's been a year since I learned about their affair and kicked him out. And it's been about eleven months and twenty-nine days since my friends became distant acquaintances. You know how it is."

Judging by the look on her face, Lydia knew exactly what Helen was talking about. They had a shared pain there, and Helen found herself really liking Lydia.

"Thanks for listening," she said. "It's

the first time I've been able to laugh about it since it happened. It feels good."

"Still, if I'd known…"

Helen laughed again. "Really, don't worry about it. Here come our salads. Relax."

They chatted over the rest of lunch and found they had a lot in common. Both enjoyed trying serial crafts, though neither had yet tried pottery. They both enjoyed camping, hiking and aquacise. Lydia had an easy laugh and a kind heart, and by the end of their meal, she'd made Helen feel like a friend. Lydia didn't have the shared history, secrets, pain, and joy Helen had with Jill, but she was funny and interesting and… Well, just not being Jill played in Lydia's favor.

Helen could start over with a friend like this

"So what do you think of Sunshine Bay?" Lydia asked.

"I like it. It's larger than Duncan, so I can be more anonymous, and there's a lot to do."

"You could start over here, you think?"

"Maybe."

"Have you dated much since your husband… left?"

"No. A few dinners, maybe, and some people—those friends with husbands—suggested I try a dating site, but I don't really want to do that. I've heard that most men my age are interested in women your age anyway."

"Well, I know one man who's interested in a woman your age."

"What do you mean?"

"Joe Brooks. He watched you pretty closely last night at the meeting."

"I don't know about that. I think he's still hung up on his ex-wife."

"Well…" Lydia leaned forward. "Let

me tell you a little story, and you be the judge. I was at Sylvia's place a few weeks ago, and I heard Jack, Sylvia's husband, talking to Joe. He was singing Sylvia's praises—the man loves her to bits. Anyway, they were talking, and Jack told Joe that he should be dating. Of course, my ears pricked up." She sat back. "Don't judge me. I rarely eavesdrop, but..."

"I'm not judging," Helen quickly assured her. If she'd overheard a man she was interested in, well, she might listen too.

"Anyway," Lydia said, leaning forward again, "Joe said that he *would* date if he could find a woman his own age. Then they talked about how younger women just didn't interest them. That made me happy because I thought he was close to my age. Imagine my shock yesterday when he told us his son was in his thirties. I mean, the man is hot. I had no idea he was so old."

Helen laughed. "Yes, so old."

"Sorry, I didn't mean it that way. I mean, I thought he was at least ten or fifteen years younger than that."

"He is, as you say, hot," Helen agreed.

"Well, after I figured out how old he was, I started watching him yesterday. And he couldn't keep his eyes from straying to you."

"Me?"

"Yes. You got up to help Sylvia with something, and he watched you leave. He kept glancing over at you when people were speaking. I know an interested man when I see one."

"Well, I'm not sure about that. Besides, I don't live here."

"Not yet. I'm hoping that by the end of the month I can talk you into relocating. I need someone to take pottery lessons with."

"Well, if I decide to move here, you'll be one of the first to know." The server brought the bill, and Helen grabbed it off the table. "I'll get this."

"You don't have to..." Lydia protested.

"I know, but I want to. And thank you for making me feel so welcome. I'm looking forward to working with you on the Tree Festival and community feast. Meanwhile, I should get home and make sure the cat's okay, and I've got a few groceries to buy before I do." She rose and put on her coat.

"Thank you for lunch, Helen. I'll see you at the next meeting." Lydia gave her a hug goodbye. It felt good—and so did the idea that Joe might be interested in her. She turned away and walked toward the car with a huge grin on her face.

CHAPTER 9

The following morning, Joe got up a little earlier than normal to cook breakfast. He would be neighborly, he decided. He could cook for other committee members without it getting awkward. Besides, he had to keep up his skills. Other than Zac and Nicole, it had been a long time since he'd cooked for anyone.

When Helen came to the door, the room was filled with breakfast smells, a broccoli and Brie quiche was warming in the oven, and the coffee was ready. Neville barked and ran between him and the door, urging him to hurry. Neville looked ready to jump out of his skin with excitement when he saw that it was Helen on the doorstop.

She looked a vision with a blue scarf wrapped around her neck and a matching toque on her head.

"Well, hello there," she said, looking straight at him. Then she turned her gaze toward Neville. "Sit." The little dog quickly wiggled onto his haunches, straining to stay in that position, watching her in anticipation. Joe looked between the two of them with amusement. She had the little devil dancing to her tune. Helen took a dog treat from her pocket and gave it to Neville. "Good boy."

"Come in. Have you had breakfast?"

"No, I haven't. I thought I would have it after my walk."

"Can I interest you in a plate of quiche?"

"Is that what smells so good?" She looked as though she would decline the invitation but then nodded and unbuttoned her coat. "Yes. I'd love that," she said. "I can't remember the last time I had quiche. Come, Neville."

Neville fell into line and followed her down the little hallway to the kitchen.

"You have him well trained already." Though he would follow her too if she asked him.

She laughed. "Dogs will do anything for a few treats, and he's a fast learner." She bent down to pat Neville on the head again. "Aren't you, boy? You're a smart one."

The dog wiggled all over at the praise, and Joe shook his head. "You have him wrapped around your little finger. Now, would you like coffee as well?"

"Oh, yes. I love that coffee. I even went down to the Beehive Bistro to have a latte yesterday."

"Glad I can help you feed your addiction." he dished the food onto plates and poured the coffee into two cups.

"This looks fantastic," she said, sitting down. "Thank you." Neville joined them at the table and whined.

"It's hard to ignore him when he whines like that," Joe said, taking pity on the dog and hoping to give him a bite of eggs.

"I know, but he'll learn soon, and then he'll stop."

"I hope so. Thanks for helping me with him. My hands have been full this year since Bethany left. After the year-end rush, I'll have more time to train him."

"I'm looking forward to seeing what you made for this year's tree. Sylvia sang your praises before she left. As far as she's concerned, yours is always the star of the show."

"That's nice for her to say, but this year I just hope I can execute what Bethany designed. Without her help, I'm behind this year. But don't tell Estelle. I'll manage to get it done, especially since I now have a willing dog walker. I don't know how I can thank you."

"Do you teach others to make fused glass?"

"I haven't taken on a student since Bethany started with me. I used to take on a few every year. Maybe I'll set up a class again in the spring. I need a new apprentice for the summer if I'm going to run my open houses."

"Could I help? I love all things craft related. My stained-glass lamp turned out pretty well when I took a class in that."

"You made a lamp? Did you cut the pieces yourself?" If she could cut glass half as well as she could train dogs, maybe she *could* help him.

"Of course. I took a few other classes before graduating to the lamp. I got pretty good at cutting the shapes."

"Maybe I can give you a couple of lessons this week. If you catch on, I could really use some help with the fused-glass ornaments."

"That would be fun. I'd love that. When can we start?"

"After your walk, maybe?" The sooner the better, in his opinion.

"All right. You have a deal."

"If you like the craft, maybe you'll take one of my classes in the spring. I usually offer them on the weekends. You could come up for a couple of days. Duncan isn't that far away."

"That's true, and I do love it here. I used to spend my summers here when I was a kid. Then, when my daughter was little, I sometimes rented a cabin, just the two of us. I had all summer off from teaching school, and we would spend two or three weeks here. I have happy memories of Sunshine Bay."

"You don't want to travel the world?"

"Oh, maybe a few trips here and there, but I'm a homebody. I like belonging somewhere."

"Do you like Duncan? You must have a lot of history there."

"That's the problem," she said. "It's shared history, and now that my husband has left... Let's just say I don't feel as welcome there as I once did. But it's getting easier now. It's been a year."

"Usually it's the man who has to start over after a divorce," he said. "That was my experience, anyway. Our mutual friends blamed me when she left."

"People like to blame the one who's left behind. In my case, my husband left me for... another woman." She looked away to where Neville was sitting quietly just beyond the table, waiting to be called. Watching her.

"That must have been hard," he said, putting his hand over hers. "I'm sorry you had to deal with that."

"It's not your fault. And probably not even hers. I thought our marriage was good, but..." She shrugged. "I guess I was wrong."

She pulled her hand away and took the last bite of her breakfast, then rinsed her plate in the sink and loaded it into the dishwasher. She brought out the bag of Neville's treats. "He's been good, sitting over there while we eat," she said. "Time for his reward."

Joe nodded, taking the hint. She was avoiding him. Avoiding getting too close. Maybe she wasn't interested, though he felt a connection with Helen he hadn't felt in a very long time.

"Neville, with me." The little dog ran straight toward her. "Sit." He sat, wagged his tail, and took the treat carefully.

"You have him literally eating out of your hands."

"It's easy once he learns. Now, where's his leash? The sooner I go, the sooner we can be back. You and I have some decorations to make."

"While you're gone, I'll get started. Just come to the studio when you get back." He took the leash off the nearby counter and handed it to her.

When he did, her hand brushed against his. Warmth seeped up his arm, and he wanted more of her touch. She looked up at him and paused. They were both holding the leash. He swallowed and licked his lips. Then her tongue peeked out to do the same.

He pulled the leash toward him, and she came closer, her lips parted in invitation—an invitation he was glad to accept. Leaning in, he captured her lips with his and grabbed her around the waist, pulling her close. She let go of the leash and slipped her hands around his neck, kissing him back. Meanwhile, Neville was barking at their feet, angry at not being the center of attention. Soon he was trying to wedge between them, pushing them apart. Joe reluctantly let her go, and Helen stepped back, looking a little dazed. He chuckled to himself. *Good.* He could still make a woman forget herself with his kisses.

She found her footing and stared at his lips for a few seconds before refocusing on the leash that was still in his hand. Neville continued to bark. "I think he needs to go for his walk now." She reached out for the leash, careful not to touch him again. "We'll be back soon."

"Don't take too long," he said.

"I won't." She shook her head. "We'll be back as soon as we can."

"I'll be waiting," he said, and she blushed and rushed out the door.

He picked up the remaining dishes and put them away, pausing to rub lipstick off of the rim of her coffee cup with his thumb. He hadn't known her for long, but she was already making her mark in his life in little ways like this. She made him want to clean up his house, make her breakfast, be a better trainer for Neville. If he wasn't careful, she would leave her mark on other places in his life too.

Like his heart.

ow. A man hadn't kissed her like that in years. Sam had nothing on this guy. She walked down the street, letting the dog lead, and touched her lips with her fingers. She had thought her dreams of Joe were good—until now. Real life was so much better. She thought back to what Lydia had said about Joe being interested in her. Apparently, her new friend had been right.

And she was right about something

else. Joe was hot. His lips were hot, his chest was hot where she'd touched him... and he made her hot. She left her coat unbuttoned to the cool air, hoping that would help. It wasn't a cold shower, but between that and watching Neville, she soon calmed down.

They walked toward the park today, and she got to see another facet of Sunshine Bay. But the events of the morning gave her pause. Sunshine Bay was a good escape for the holiday season, but she hadn't counted on this. Was she ready for a man in her life? Did she even have room for one?

There were so many things changing. Couldn't just one thing stay the same?

She had been test-driving Sunshine Bay the past few days, seeing if she could trade her old life in Duncan and start again from scratch. Did she want to do that? She had already given up so much.

Neville barked and strained at the leash, and she looked up just in time to see a squirrel streak past. "Oh, no you don't," she said, pulling him back. "You can't have everything you want."

The dog continued to strain at the leash until the squirrel was well out of sight. "Maybe you're right, Neville," she murmured under her breath. "Just because you can't have everything you want doesn't mean you shouldn't try." She turned back the way they'd come. "Let's go, boy. We need to get your business done and get back so I can learn fused glass."

Neville reluctantly left the foot of the tree where he had last seen the squirrel and began to walk again—until he spotted another squirrel, this one a little closer. And he was off again, pulling her toward the spot where a bushy, gray tail had disappeared into the bushes.

"Neville." She strained at the leash again. "Heel."

The dog turned and walked back toward her, wagging his tail, unapologetic about taking the initiative.

"Sylvia's right. You can be a little devil, but you're cute." And his actions reminded her of something else she had been thinking lately—or maybe it had been some platitude uttered by a well-meaning former friend. When one opportunity doesn't work out, there's always another to replace it—like Neville's squirrels. You just had to let the first one go so you could focus on the next one. "Let's get back. Joe will be waiting for us."

She repeated that to herself. *Joe will be waiting for us. For me.* It was a simple thing, really, having someone there when you returned home. Someone who would notice if you weren't there.

Someone who would care if you were late.

It was a simple thing, having someone to love.

And it meant the world.

CHAPTER 11

"You're back," said Joe, when Helen stepped into his workshop. "I thought you got lost."

"Not today. Today Neville took me squirrel hunting in the park."

"Not sure what he will do if he ever catches one." He pointed to a hook by the door. "You can hang your coat there, and over on that wall you'll find an apron you can use."

She did as he asked, and he watched her, appreciating the way she moved.

"If you come over to this workbench, there are some patterns, and some tools to cut the glass."

"I love these," she said as she flipped through the drawings. "*Crystal Rhapsody*. What a great title for it. I like the drums and flute and notes. I think this will be fun."

"Let me show you how to do the cutting first. Once we have all the pieces, we can put them together and fire them in the kiln. Let's start with the easy ones. I think the drum has the fewest lines."

He showed her how to cut out the glass and then patiently watched until she got it right. "You have good, steady hand. These will work out well, I think."

They worked side by side for an hour. She traced and cut the pieces, and he ground down the edges and prepared them for the kiln. "Once we're done this part, we have to arrange the shapes on top of these white disks I prepared the other day."

"And then you put them in the kiln. Wonderful."

"Are you okay to do this on your own for a while? I need to blow a few more globes today."

"Certainly. I'll be just fine."

"Good." He stood and squeezed her shoulder, wanting to touch her even in a friendly way, before he walked across the room and put distance between them. He needed to remove the temptation to force an unwanted kiss on her again. "We'll work until noon if that's okay, and then we can get some lunch."

She turned on the chair and looked up, resting her hand on his arm. "Thank you for teaching me this. I loved my stained-glass classes. I used to take all my craft classes with my best friend, but she hated the glass class. I would never have gotten her to do this."

"You're doing me a favor," he said, waiting, not wanting to move while her hand was on his arm, not wanting to move while she was looking at him that way, like she wanted something...

She stood then, stepping away from the stool and toward him. No further words were necessary as she wrapped her arms around his neck and brought her lips to his. And something inside him exploded. He grasped her around the waist and lifted her onto the end of the workbench, stepping between her legs, removing every inch of air between them. A perfect fusion.

They kissed a long time, until an alarm went on his phone. The annoying sound just kept going. He had set it up like that for a reason, so he would remember to walk Neville or check the furnace or the kiln. Reluctantly, he stepped away. There was a lot of work to do today. Maybe they could continue this tonight when there were no interruptions.

"We should probably get to work now," he said, and she simply nodded. Her lips, red from their kisses, made him want to kiss her again. He gave in to the temptation one more time when the alarm slipped into a snooze mode.

Then the noise began again, and she laughed. "Duty calls."

"Unfortunately. Maybe we can explore this further tonight?"

"I'd like that."

"Well, let's get back to work, then." He walked over to the furnace to begin the green globes, being careful to focus on the molten glass rather than the hot woman across the room.

As they worked, they fell into an easy

conversation. He told her about things to do in the area. She told him about her daughter and about her trip to Ottawa the year before. "I had never been there, so I thought I would see the nation's capital. I loved the museum and the art gallery. Some of these pieces," she said, pointing at the shelves that lined the end wall, "look like the ones in the gift shop there."

"Some of my work was there once upon a time," he said. "I worked in a studio in Ontario before I came out here to live. Maeve wanted to watch whales, and so we came to where the whales lived. And then she decided she didn't want to watch orca but hunt for blue whales instead."

"Do you regret leaving Ontario?"

"No. This was a great place to raise Zac, and we have far better weather. And I was able to build my studio, make my own hours. I like it here. It suits me."

"I can see that," she said.

"You mentioned earlier that you weren't sure where you would be in the spring. Are you thinking of moving?"

"Once I get divorced," she said, "I'll have to sell the house as part of the settlement. Then I'll need to decide."

"When will that happen?" he asked, and then wished he hadn't. Did he really want to know the answer?

"Oh. Soon. Once all the paperwork is done."

She looked sad, and he didn't like it.

"I found that part to be hard. Especially since she wanted it done as quickly as possible so she could be free to marry again. It took me a long time to get over it, but once I forgave her, I was able to move on."

"How did you forgive her?" she asked.

"Well," he said, blowing into the tube to make another green globe, "when you have kids together, it's harder. You can't just make a clean break. I didn't want my son in the middle of a constant fight, and when I thought it all through, I realized we were better off without her. You can't hold someone who doesn't want to be held, and you can't move on if you don't let them go."

"So you're saying that if you don't forgive, you end up stuck?"

"Yes, exactly." He turned the globe, polishing it with a stack of paper made for that purpose, on the bench where he was working. "You end up stuck in a purgatory of sorts, where you can't move forward because you can't let go of what you didn't really have in the first place."

"Like Neville's squirrels," she said.

"Neville's squirrels?"

"He can only chase one at a time. He has to let one go if he's going to pursue another one."

"Though in Neville's case, it isn't for lack of trying."

"True," she laughed, and he was happy to hear that laughter. He wanted nothing more than to hear it again and again. He hoped her husband would finish the paperwork for their divorce soon and let her go so she could move on. He didn't like seeing her suffer the long wait.

CHAPTER 12

The next several days went by quickly. Helen spent time phoning the local businesses to confirm food donations and organize the volunteers for both events. Every few days, she met one or more of the committee members to compare notes, go over the list of tasks, and celebrate every item they checked off as they went.

Most mornings she walked Neville and helped Joe in the shop, learning how to fuse glass and making the decorations.

At night, she would visit Joe and watch television, take Neville through his training, and snuggle close to Joe. She felt comfortable. Like she belonged there.

Like she belonged with him.

∿

A week before the festival, they were working in the shop when a text notification sounded on Helen's phone. She glanced at the screen, said, "Excuse me a minute," and stepped outside.

Joe waited a few minutes, and when she didn't return, he grabbed their coats and followed her. When he got outside, the sun was in the west; it was getting late, and he would have to take Neville for his walk soon. But first, he had to find her. It was getting cold.

He heard her voice coming from

around the corner of the studio. He followed the sound to find her talking into the phone with tears on her face. She looked angry. Or was it sad? He couldn't tell, but he had to see if he could help.

"Why did you involve Kim?" she said into the phone. "You've ruined all my other relationships. Why not that one, too? Is that it?"

Joe watched her swipe at her eyes with her left hand. "It's not like she doesn't have enough to deal with without worrying about her parents. I told you, I'll do it when I'm ready."

Joe walked closer, making himself known, and she turned toward him, her face blotchy from tears, beautiful as ever. He silently handed her coat to her, and she smiled wanly, mouthed thank you, then let him help her into her coat while she listened to the voice on the other end.

Finally, she said, "I'll think about it. I

have to go now." With that, she clicked the phone off and turned toward Joe. "Thank you for bringing me my coat."

"You're shivering. Come here." He slowly drew her close, and she came without hesitation. He wrapped his arms around her, holding her closer to him, and they melted into the embrace like the fusing of two pieces of glass, different but necessary to make the whole more beautiful. He wanted her to stay there. He wanted her to be part of his life. Wanted to always be the one she turned to for comfort. She was no longer shivering but shaking, and he realized she was crying.

He grasped her shoulders and bent down to look at her. "What happened? Can I help?"

"Divorce. It's just so hard."

"I know, but once you get the paperwork, you can sign it off and start to move on. Is that what you were talking about?" He didn't want to pry, but he wanted to know. If the man wasn't following through on the paperwork, maybe he wanted her back. Joe didn't think he could deal with that again. Not now that he loved her.

He hugged her closer as he let the words sink into his brain.

He loved her.

"It's not Sam," she said. "Well, not normally, though today I'm angry with him because he phoned my daughter and asked her if she knew where I was and why I hadn't signed the divorce papers." She turned to him. "Then she texted to let me know about the call, and I phoned him to tell him off. I was angry that he would bring her into it. It's not her marriage."

"You have the divorce papers? Why haven't you signed them?"

So Helen was the one who wanted to stay married. What did that mean for him? For them? He would listen, hear her out, not jump to conclusions. Maybe it was something about the financial settlement she didn't like.

"I phoned and told him not to involve Kim anymore, and he promised he wouldn't. He's a lovely man. Good father. He was even a good husband for a long time, but our marriage hasn't worked in years. It started really falling apart when Kim left home."

Why was she so angry? People didn't get angry about things or people they didn't care about.

"Then why are you having trouble signing the divorce papers?"

She didn't answer, just sobbed harder.

"I can't help if I don't understand."

"I told you he left me for another woman?"

"That's hard, but it doesn't reflect on

you. It just means you had outgrown the relationship."

"He left me for my best friend." She gasped for breath, and the sobs grew heavier.

"I didn't know. I'm sorry."

"All our other friends took their side. Couples always seem to win over singles in these situations."

"And you think if you refuse to sign the papers, you'll get your friend back?" he didn't understand how that would work.

She withdrew from his embrace and stood back, and he regretted his question immediately. She walked a little way toward the studio, away from him.

After a long moment, she said, "At first I was doing it for revenge. You know. You take everything from me; I'll keep what you want from you. But revenge isn't really as sweet as they say." She turned toward him again. "I realized that if I sign the papers, I have to admit she's gone too. That they *both* chose each other over me. And that I am being forced to leave the only town I've known for my adult life. Where I raised my daughter. Where I grew up. Do you know what it's like to be shunned?"

He approached her, trying to get back the closeness. "In my experience, you can think of things like this two ways."

"What do you mean?" She stopped, moving let him get closer.

"You can think of yourself as being forced to leave, or you can think of it as outgrowing a place and finding a somewhere new you want to be. No one is *making* you leave Duncan, you know. You could ride it out and keep living there."

"Yes, that's true. At least until I find a better alternative."

"Maybe Sunshine Bay could be your

better alternative." He pulled her closer and kissed her, putting all his hopes into that kiss, willing her to see a way to a future here. "Maybe staying with me could be your future."

She kissed him back, and he gathered her closer. This was right. She was right. Now all he needed to do was convince her. "So, are you ready to sign the divorce papers now?" he asked between kisses. "To stay here?"

His words hung in the cold air, and she stepped back again—back and away. "Why does everyone want me to sign those papers? I want to do it when I want to do it. Not on anyone else's schedule."

"Why are you holding on? Don't you want a life here? Don't you want to see where this can go?"

"I can't stay here and be forced to do what I don't want to do."

"I'm not forcing you to do anything.

I'm asking you to choose me. Let go and choose me. I love you."

He watched her face, eyes bloodshot from crying, turn from sadness to anger to ice.

"I have to go." And she turned and walked up the path, taking his heart with her.

CHAPTER 13

*H*elen stalked back to Sylvia's house, let herself in, flopped on the couch, and closed her eyes. How could Joe tell her he loved her right in the middle of their first fight? And why was he pushing her to sign those papers? If he really loved her, he should be on her side. He should try to see it through her eyes. He should—

"Oomph." She opened her eyes to find Angel sitting on her lap, looking at her. "Hello. How are you doing?"

Angel blinked slowly and allowed Helen to stroke her fur.

"Thank you for visiting me. Are you worried about me? You're right. I shouldn't be crying, but what am I going to do?"

Angel responded by curling up on her lap and purring like a small engine. "Well, you're not much help. All you do is sleep."

Or maybe she was helping. This cat had been a rescue—alone in the world, from what Sylvia had told her. And now here she was, interacting with people, making new friends, and content with her new life. Even Angel had found it in her little cat self to trust Sylvia. To believe things could get better if she let go of living in a park and moved into a house.

Helen slid down so she could lie on the couch. Maybe if she took a catnap like Angel did, she could gain perspective. But sleep stayed out of reach as her mind galloped through all that had happened over the past year. She thought of the betrayal, the anger, and her fear of starting over. The fear of letting go. Of giving up on what she had to grab for something new. How could she find the strength to do that?

She continued to stroke the cat, and Angel continued to purr. Could she do it? Move to a new town and start again? She had some friends here now, and she had her volunteer work, and she could probably find some teaching or tutoring work. Even if it didn't work out with Joe, Sunshine Bay was large enough that she wouldn't be in a fishbowl this time. She wouldn't be judged by everyone she met and found wanting.

"You know what, Angel? You were right to take a risk and come to live with Sylvia. Maybe I should do that too."

The cat was now purring loudly, as

though in agreement.

"I mean, what am I really sacrificing? This year has been horrid and empty, and if I came here, there would be a lot to gain —friends, new activities, new hobbies."

And if Joe was telling the truth, she would gain a life of love.

There was really only one way to find out.

Angel continued to purr, and Helen let her. It had taken several days, but the cat was finally getting used to her, and she relished the closeness. The warmth.

What did she want?

Right now, she wanted—needed—to go home. "Sorry about this," she said to Angel as she shifted the cat onto the sofa. She went into the kitchen to make sure there was enough cat food and water for at least a day. If she stayed home longer, she was sure Lydia would be able to feed Angel. Sylvia would understand.

CHAPTER 14

*T*he hall was filled with families, and more noise than Joe was normally comfortable with, but this afternoon he wanted human contact. It had been a whole twenty-four hours since he had last seen Helen, and when he arrived at the hall, Estelle told him Helen had an emergency to deal with and might not make it to the auction.

Instead of thinking about her, he focused on the children. They were moving from activity to activity, getting their faces painted, working on paper crafts, and listening to a new story being told by Misty the Story Maven, a young woman who had gone to school with Zac. She was a good actress and storyteller, and both he and the children were captivated by her tales.

Joe was taking his turn at the tree table, selling raffle tickets for the baskets arranged on a shelf behind him. People were admiring the trees, which were tucked behind a fence so no one could knock them over accidentally—the official line—or take some of the baubles home in their pockets—the unofficial line.

"Did you design that tree, Joe?" He looked away from Misty the Story Maven to find Raymond Charles, a man in his late sixties. The same man who had commissioned the blue vase. Raymond was dressed as though he were going to a formal dinner rather than an afternoon community event.

"I had a part in it. This year my assistant designed it, and I also had help with the fused pieces. It was a team effort."

Raymond waved his hand at the tree. "I told Carl that it must have come from your studio. He wants to bid on that one, and I expect we'll be opening our wallets as wide as it takes to win."

"It's all for a good cause," said Joe.

"Two good causes," Raymond said, glancing over at Carl, a well-dressed man with silver hair who was talking animatedly to a friend.

"Two?"

"The hospital, of course," said Raymond, giving Carl a secret smile, "and my marriage." He turned to the table and pulled a book of raffle tickets toward him. "If there is anything I have learned from my trail of failed relationships, it is that marriages, at least the good ones, take work. I'll do pretty much anything to keep that man happy."

"And it looks to be well worth your effort," Joe said, when he saw how Carl smiled back at Raymond.

"Yes. Thank you again for all your effort in making that vase so many times."

"Anything for a satisfied customer."

"I know you are just being kind," said Raymond. "But thank you." He handed Joe the entire booklet of tickets and a twenty-dollar bill to cover the cost.

"Thank you," said Joe. "And good luck with the raffle."

Raymond nodded and returned to his partner, who took him by the hand and pulled him into the circle of conversation. What he wouldn't give for Helen to be here right now, and for her to be the one to take him by the hand. She had made him want to be part of things again, and he missed her.

Estelle came a few minutes later to relieve him at the table, and he moved to the edge of the room to people-watch, wishing again that Helen were here. She would have loved this, but she had her own life, and he had no idea when, or if, he would see her again.

"It's a good turnout this year," a voice said from beside him.

"Hi, Lydia." He turned his head to acknowledge her and then turned back to the crowd.

"I was wondering if you could tell me something," she said.

"Sure, if I can," he said cautiously. He shifted his weight to the foot farthest from her, in an attempt to create some distance. His throat tightened as he considered how best to let her down, to tell her he wasn't interested.

"See that man over there talking to Shane, my son?" She nodded toward a man in a conductor's cap talking to a young boy. "Do you know him?"

"That's Tyler. He works with Jack at the park. I think he's the one driving the holiday train this year while Jack's away."

"Ah, that would explain the hat," she said, "and why my son is commandeering his time. Shane is mad about trains. His grandfather used to work for CP Rail."

"That would explain it, yes."

"Do you know anything more about him?"

He suddenly noticed the interested gleam in her eye and realized that she didn't see Tyler as a man she needed to rescue from her son's questions, but as a man full stop. Lucky Tyler.

"If memory serves, he's a mechanic. And I'm not sure, but I think he's single. Jack mentioned that he and his girlfriend broke up a few weeks ago."

"Interesting," said Lydia. "By the way, I approve."

"Approve of what?" She was still watching her son and Tyler having an animated conversation. Maybe she approved of the way Tyler was treating her son.

"I like Helen. She's nice. It would be really nice if she moved here."

"She's got her life in Duncan. I doubt she'd leave all that to come here."

"I think she's considering big changes."

"I don't know where you get your information. She's still married, and she's not even here."

"I don't think it would take much for her to leave that life behind. Not if she found somewhere to belong—and maybe someone to belong to."

He scowled. "She didn't even follow through on her volunteer time today."

"I wouldn't be so sure about that."

"What's that supposed to mean?" This was an exasperating conversation. He turned toward her again, but she wasn't there to answer him. Instead, she was halfway across the room, hurrying while trying to act casual. Tyler didn't stand a chance.

He frowned and turned back to people-watching. If they hadn't asked him to fill Helen's time slot at the raffle table, he would have left by now. He glanced at his watch. It was almost time to walk back to the table. Might as well get it over with.

He turned and noticed a woman walking ahead of him. A woman with auburn hair. His heart skipped. She was here. He should have been angry, but he was too relieved to see her.

She turned to him as he approached and walked to the side of the room where there was a little privacy. He followed, just as Neville would.

"I'm sorry I left the way I did. I was angry, and I had to figure some things out," she said without preamble. "And I was ashamed at the way I'd been acting toward Jill and, yes, even Sam."

"Ashamed? Ashamed of what?"

"I was so angry at them leaving me out in the cold that I wasn't thinking about their feelings, or about how the situation must be affecting Kim."

"It takes a long time to forgive a betrayal like that." He was speaking in a low voice, and he was close enough now to touch her. Oh, how he wanted to touch her. "It took me years to forgive Maeve."

"I know. But you were right. Lydia was right. Even Neville was right."

"Neville?"

"I can't move on if I don't let go. So I signed the papers, and I drove to Duncan this morning to give them to Sam."

"You did that?"

"Yes. And then I listed my house and left Sam in charge of showing it."

He reached for her and rubbed his hands on her arms, itching to pull her close, kiss her, jump with joy. Was she saying what he thought she was saying?

"Jill cried and told me it was the best present I could have given them," she said. "And you know what? I didn't feel resentment this time. Only relief at being able to make someone's life better. Relief at being able to help two people who are very much in love. Relief that I could still be her friend."

"And now what are you going to do?"

"Well, I was hoping you might help me figure that out." She raised her arms and placed them around his neck, and he pulled her close, turning his back to the crowded room. "You promised me once that you'd show me around this town. And since my heart seems to be here now, I thought I would take you up on it."

"You're moving here?"

"Yes, once I find a place to move to, and once the house sells. If I don't get on as a teacher on call, I can always tutor a few hours a week."

"You're sure about this?"

"I've never been surer of anything in my entire life. I want to start over in Sunshine Bay. With you. I love you, Joe. I never thought I would find love again, and there you were, hiding in Sunshine Bay."

"I love you too." He bent his head and kissed her, fusing his lips to hers, forgetting the people behind them. He had to agree with Jill. Having Helen here, ready to start a new life with him in it, was the best present he could have received this year.

Or any year.

EPILOGUE

Joe closed the studio and locked the door, tucking a small box into his pocket. He stopped at the run and smiled at Neville, who jumped up to greet him. Since Zac and Nicole had returned from Nicaragua a few months before, he had missed the little dog. He was tickled when Neville came to visit this time.

"Are you ready?" he asked the dog, walking over to open the door and let him out. "She'll be here soon."

Neville greeted him in the exuberant way only a dog can. Then he bounded along ahead of him, straining at the leash, as though he knew where they were going. Joe opened the car door, and the dog jumped up into the back seat, barking at him to hurry.

The weather was turning again, just as it had the year he and Helen met. For many, winter was a time for death and dying. Hibernation. Sleep. But he thought of it as the time when she had brought love and meaning back into his life.

He switched on the radio as he drove south along the Island Highway. He hoped they hadn't delayed her plane. She had been out in Ontario visiting her daughter for the past two weeks, and they'd been the longest two weeks of his life.

The airport was coming up on the left-hand side of the road, and he searched the sky for a plane. The sky was empty but for gray clouds full of the snow that was forecast to fall any minute, dashing any hope that he would see her today.

He pulled into a parking stall in front of the tiny airport, plugged the meter with a loonie, and walked inside, scanning the room for the notification board to see if the plane was still expected to land. The room was full of travelers waiting to board their planes—a good sign. That meant that they hadn't officially canceled any flights yet. He walked up to the counter to ask about Helen's flight and was told the plane had taken off from Toronto and would land soon.

Instead of waiting inside, he fetched Neville from the car to take him for a walk. It would give Neville some exercise, and it would give Joe something to do instead of stare at the television screen, waiting for the listing to say "arrived." This way he could watch the plane land.

The little Westie ran ahead of him and along the fence that lined the runway. Waiting. Watching. Nothing came, and the only plane on the runway now had a thin dusting of snow on the wings. This wasn't good. What if they redirected the plane to Vancouver? They would have to wait hours more while she got a bus or cab to the ferry and then made the crossing.

Thinking of that, he took out his phone and googled the ferry schedule to see if there were any alerts. If the wind was too strong, she would have to stay in Vancouver until at least tomorrow. A gust of wind played at his scarf, blowing it up in front of his face, and he pulled it down again while he stared at the screen. Weather had delayed the ferries. It was a real possibility that she wouldn't make it home on time.

He tamped down his disappointment and dialed her number. He could at least make sure she had a place to stay tonight. He needed to know she was warm, dry, safe. He held the phone to his ear, and it rang a few times before going to voicemail.

Maybe she was on the plane, and it would land soon. He should put Neville back in the car where he had a blanket to curl up on. Then he could get back to the terminal and warm up.

"Come on, Neville. Let's go back to the car." He turned and tugged at the leash, expecting Neville to follow slowly behind as he had been trained to do. Instead, the little Westie yelped and ran ahead, pulling the leash out of his hand. "Neville!" he yelled. "Come back here." The little dog raced ahead, and he ran after him, hoping the dog wouldn't chase after a car or go out on the road.

"Neville!"

Neville ran toward a crowd of people emerging from the terminal—likely those who'd learned their flights had been canceled. Some were hailing cabs, and others climbed onto the nearby bus. Where had Neville gone?

Joe couldn't see him anywhere, but he could hear him. He was yelping in that way he did when he recognized someone, and it sounded like he had stopped running. With every step Joe took, Neville's bark got louder.

And then Joe saw him, sitting beside a bright-red suitcase and looking up adoringly at Helen, who was holding Neville's leash, watching Joe walk toward her, and grinning in that way that lit up his life.

She was here.

"When did you get here?" he asked.

"I got the earlier flight. I was afraid they would stop flying when I heard the forecast."

"Why didn't you call?"

"I only arrived half an hour ago, and I knew you would be here soon."

"Well, thank goodness. It looks like they've canceled the ferries."

"Yes, and the flights. I feel bad for all those people who have to turn around and go back home now."

"Come here, you," he said, enveloping her in a warm hug. "I've missed you."

"I've missed you too," she said. "Happy anniversary."

"You did remember."

"How could I forget the first day I met you?"

"Oh, that reminds me. I have something for you."

"What?"

"Come. Let's get your bag and this

little devil into the car first. It's cold out here."

He grasped the handle of her suitcase and pulled it toward the car while Helen focused on navigating Neville along the sidewalk and past the line of people still waiting for a ride home.

After settling into the car, he pulled the box from his pocket and handed it to her. "I always thought this type of thing was too sentimental, but that was before I knew you."

"What is it?" She giggled, and he smiled. He loved the way the little things in life delighted her.

"First, I have a bit of a story. Last year, when I met you, I was making a vase for a couple. They had both been married before, and they wanted to celebrate their union with a traditional anniversary gift. That was their third anniversary, and so it would be glass or crystal. And because their wedding colors were blue and white, they wanted something in cobalt blue."

"Oh, I remember. You were making it when I first saw you in the studio."

"Yes, though I had to make two more after that before they were satisfied. They were the most difficult couple to please."

"I guess they wanted it to be perfect," she said.

"Yes. Anyway, until I met you, I thought a tradition of commissioning blue gifts to mark their anniversary was the most saccharine thing I had ever heard of. But now... Well, let's just say I can see the benefits."

"And this is something along those lines?" she asked, holding the box between them.

"Well, I was thinking about how we met last year and the things that brought us together. I wanted to commemorate it. Start our own tradition."

"Okay..."

"Open it. I hope you like it. If you do, I'm going to make you one every year."

She looked at the box and then up at him. "I love you so much," she said.

"I love you too. Now go on, open it."

She slipped the red ribbon from the simple white box and looked inside. "Oh, my goodness."

"Do you like it?"

"I love it!" she said, looking down at the glass tree ornament he had fashioned just for her. It was an evergreen tree decorated with red and white and silver dots. On the top, where an angel would normally sit, there was a black cat wearing a red ribbon around her throat. A little white Westie was sitting at the base of the tree, looking out at Helen. "It's perfect. I already love this new tradition."

"Not half as much as I love you." He

pulled her close and kissed her until she pushed back a bit.

"I think we should go home now. We have a lot of catching up to do."

Yap, yap, came a dog voice from the back seat.

Joe laughed and started the car. "Home it is."

And the trio drove back down the highway through the falling snow, glad to be together again.

THANK YOU

Dear Reader,

Thank you for reading Angel and the Neville Next Door, the third Sunshine Bay story. I hope it gave you some joy.

To be the first to learn about the next Sunshine Bay story take a moment to go to my website at JeanineLauren.com to sign up for my newsletter.

If you enjoyed the story, please consider taking a few minutes to leave a review. Reviews are a fabulous way to support authors so we can continue to write more books for you to enjoy.

Until next time, happy reading.

Jeanine Lauren

ABOUT THE AUTHOR

Jeanine Lauren has always loved a good story. She prefers those where the strength of community and the power of love combine to overcome even the darkest of situations.

Jeanine writes from her home in the lower mainland of British Columbia, Canada, not far from the fictional town of Sunshine Bay, where many of her characters live.

Angel and the Neville Next Door is Jeanine's third book.

Printed in Great Britain
by Amazon